TH
LO

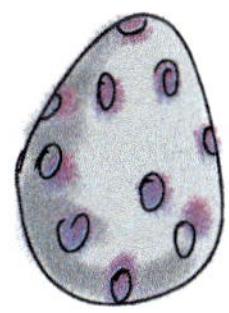

By Paul Smith

Illustrations by Steven Smith

Dedicated to Bailey Paul Smith.

Inspired by my Grandchildren

A small Sparrow one day found a little egg.

It was a small egg, grey in colour with purple spots all over it.

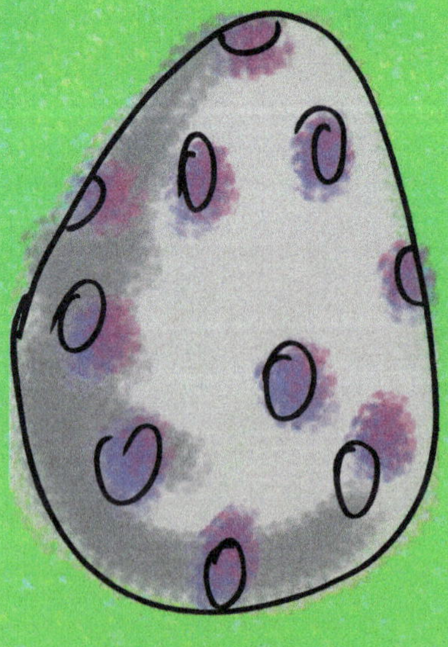

The Sparrow picked up the egg
and thought to herself,
“that looks like a Blackbirds egg.
I’ll take it to the Blackbird”

The small Sparrow took the egg to the Blackbirds nest and put it in along with the other eggs and flew away.

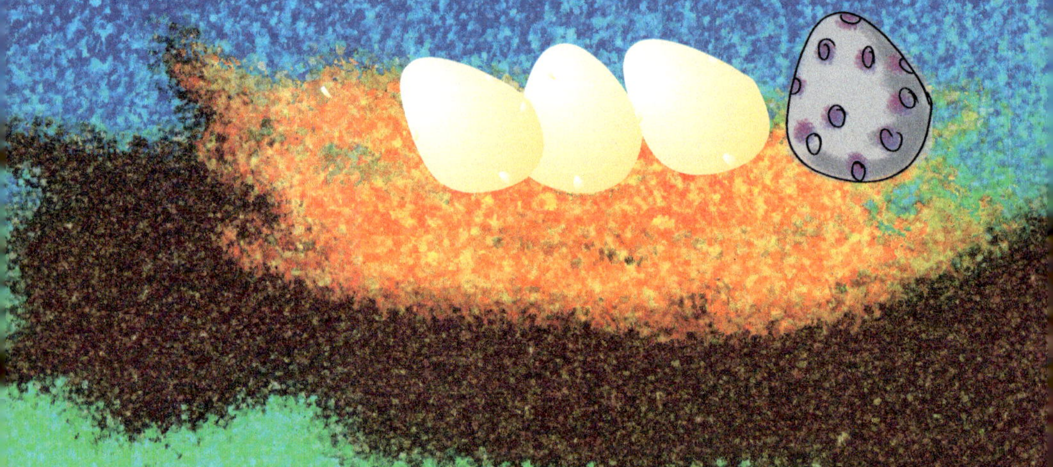

When the Blackbird came back to the nest it sat on the eggs to keep them warm.

During the night the little egg shook a bit, wobbled a bit and got a little bit **bigger.**

In the morning the
Blackbird looked at her eggs
and thought,
“That's not a Blackbird egg,
it must be a Chicken egg?”

The Blackbird picked up the egg and took it to the Chickens.

It gave the egg to a Chicken who put it with her other eggs, then sat on them to keep them warm.

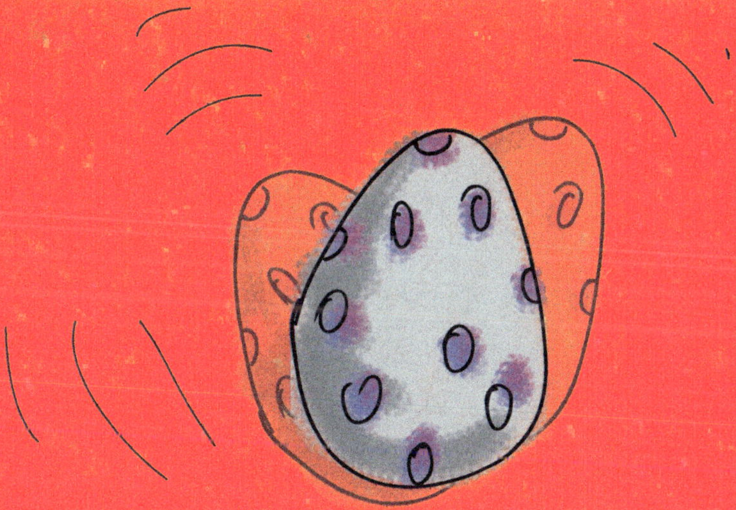

Whilst the egg was warm,
it shook a bit, wobbled a bit and
then got a little bit **bigger.**

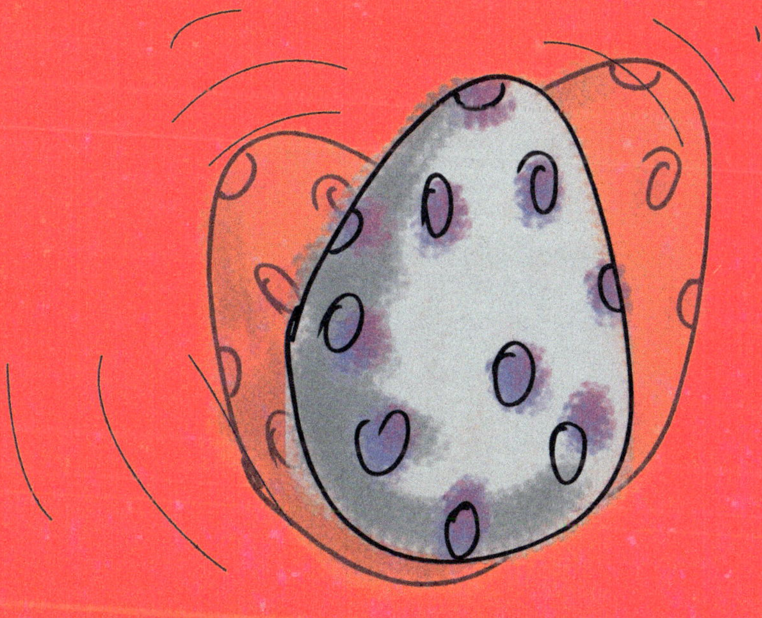

In the morning the Chicken looked at the egg and thought,

"That's not a Chicken egg it must belong to an Ostrich?"

The Chicken took the egg to the Ostrich and said
"This egg is too big for a Chicken it must belong to you"

The Ostrich took her head out of the sand.

Then placed the egg in the nest along with all the others.

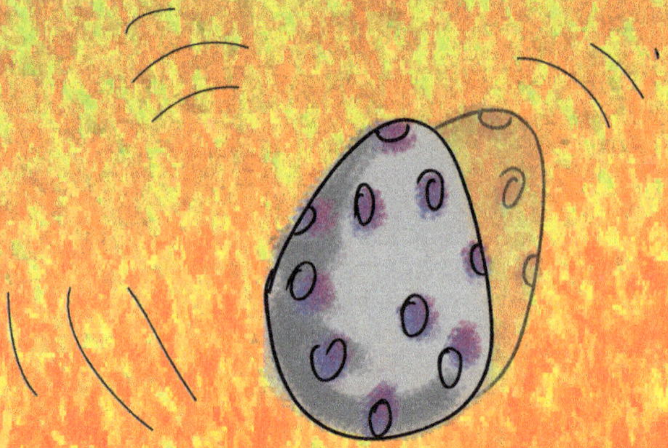

She sat on the egg to keep it warm.
Then went to sleep. During the
night the little egg shook a bit,
wobbled a bit and
then got a little bit **bigger**.

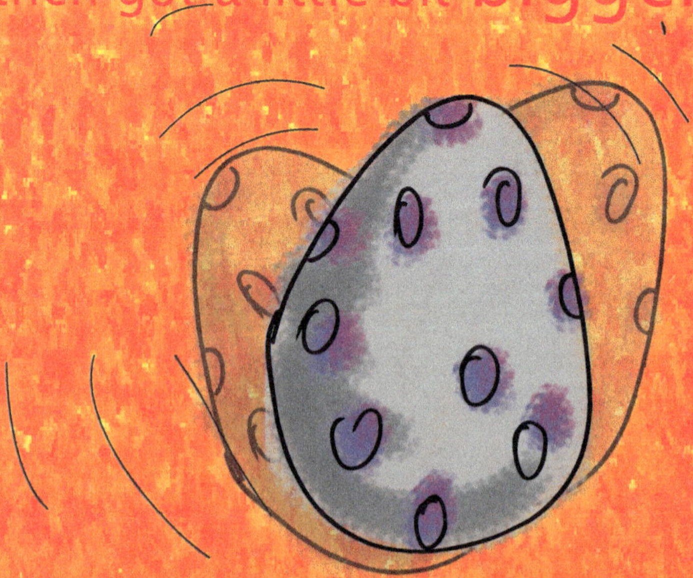

In the morning the Ostrich was
amazed to see that the egg had
grown to such a size.
She scratched her head and thought,

“that's not an Ostrich egg,
it must be a Lizard egg.”

The Ostrich took the egg to the Lizard, who was sat on a rock.

" I have this egg that is too big for an Ostrich it must belong too a Lizard?"

The Lizard flicked out her tongue
and said
" That looks like a Lizard egg.
I will look after it."

The Lizard buried the egg in the sand and wrapped her long tail over the top of the egg and went to sleep.

During the night the little egg shook a bit, wobbled a bit and then got a little bit **bigger.**

In the morning the Lizard saw how
big the egg had become,
flicked out her tongue
and thought "that's too big for
a Lizard egg.
It must be a Crocodile egg"

The Lizard took the
egg to the
Crocodile
down by the river and said.

"this egg is too big for a
Lizard it must belong to a
Crocodile?"

The Crocodile took one look at the now quite large egg and smiled "It sure looks like a Crocodile egg."

The Croc placed the egg alongside the others in her nest then settled down for the night.

In the morning the crocodile was awoken by a

CRACKING

sound.

She looked at the egg and saw it wobble a little bit, shake a little bit......

It wobbled a bit more, then shook some more and a large crack began to appear down the side.

The not quite so little
egg began to
break open.

Out of the egg popped the strangest creature the Crocodile had ever seen.

It had a beak like a Chicken

a head like a Blackbird......

feet like a Sparrow

and a tail like
a Lizard

It's body looked like
an Ostrich
and it was
covered in
scales like
a Crocodile..

It was a

Dinosaur.!!!!

The little dinosaur let out a small cry "**YYEEOOOWWWW!!!**"

The Crocodile was quite amazed by this and thought "I will take this baby to find it's mummy"

She picked up the baby and carried it to the caves at the edge of the mountain.

She called out to the Dinosaur who came running and said "Have you found my Little Lost Egg?"

The Crocodile replied "Yes I believe I have"

" I got it from the Lizard,
who was given it by the Ostrich,
who received it from the Chicken,
who got it from the Blackbird,
who discovered it in her nest
after the Sparrow found it
by the big tree!"

"That's where I left it" gasped
the Dinosaur.
"Thank you very much"

Now the Little Lost Egg was not lost anymore.

The End

Lightning Source UK Ltd.
Milton Keynes UK
UKOW06f0432090517
300802UK00011B/52/P

9 781782 225003